Shane Hawley   —   Joel Erkkinen

© 2018 by Shane Hawley & Joel Erkkinen

Published by Button Poetry / Exploding Pinecone Press
Minneapolis, MN 55403 | http://www.buttonpoetry.com

All Rights Reserved

Manufactured in Canada

ISBN 978-1-943735-46-4

WARNING! MANY FICTIONAL CHILDREN WERE KILLED IN THE MAKING OF THIS BOOK!

A Note to Parents

Take the following multiple-choice test to determine if this book is for you and yours:

A. You love Tim Burton movies and couldn't wait to share them with your kids, so you did when they were infants.
B. Tim Burton movies scare and confuse you. Why would anyone watch them, let alone show them to their children?

A. You would do anything to protect your children from harm, even if it meant broaching a subject that was scary or uncomfortable.
B. You don't talk about bad things in your family because denial is the best method of survival.

A. If it's within reach on your bookshelves, your kids are allowed to read it.
B. You are not teaching your precious angels to read — it might pollute their minds.

If you picked A for **ANY** of the choices above, this book is right up your alley.

If you picked B for **ALL** of the choices above, this may not be the book for you. A laser printer manual or Ikea instructions might be more to your liking.

Joel would like to thank Sarah, Greta, Gavin, and all his family and friends for support and for helping to foster his slightly odd sense of humor.

Shane would like to thank Anitra, Ava, Brenna, Bria, Dragonlord, Isaac, Jack, Kieran, Peyton, and all the other little monsters that inspired him to write a "children's book."

Both creators would like to thank all the stupid people who died in stupid ways to make this book a possibility. We couldn't have done it without you.

A
is for Alligator

Alligators will kill you.

Since 1973 there have been 31 fatal alligator attacks, 27 of them in Florida.
Florida is a terrible place to die.

Remember that when you get old.

B

is for Bull

Bulls will kill you.

Bulls have killed 533 bullfighters in Spain since 1700, which is fine because, like all little men with something to prove, bullfighters deserve what's coming to them.

C is for Cow

Cows will kill you.

Eating beef from cows with mad cow disease has killed 229 people. Somewhere in cow heaven, millions of innocent cheeseburgers are laughing.

D is for Dolphin

Dolphins will kill you.

In 1994, a wild bottlenose dolphin rammed a drunk man who was physically harassing it. He died later that day of internal injuries, which served him right

Elephants will kill you.

Elephants are responsible for hundreds of human deaths each year, often when raiding crops or decimating villages in search of alcohol. Elephants are bigger, meaner drunks than Santa Claus.

Frogs will kill you.

A poison dart frog is two centimeters long and has enough poison in its tiny body to kill 10 adult men. It has enough hate in its heart to kill millions.

Goonches will kill you.

A giant goonch catfish is suspected to have eaten three people in India. It weighs anywhere from 200 to 300 pounds and is very angry at humans for naming it a goonch.

H
is for Hornet

Hornets will kill you.

In the summer of 2013, the Asian giant hornet killed at least 42 people in China. At almost two inches long with a sting that causes organ failure, the Asian giant hornet is absolute proof that if God exists, he hates humans.

I
is for
Inland Taipan

Inland Taipans will kill you.

The inland taipan's bite contains enough venom in each strike to kill at least 100 adult men or 400 six-year-olds. Its venom is specially adapted to kill warm-blooded animals, like all of your friends.

Don't Forget Your Milk!

Jellyfish will kill you.

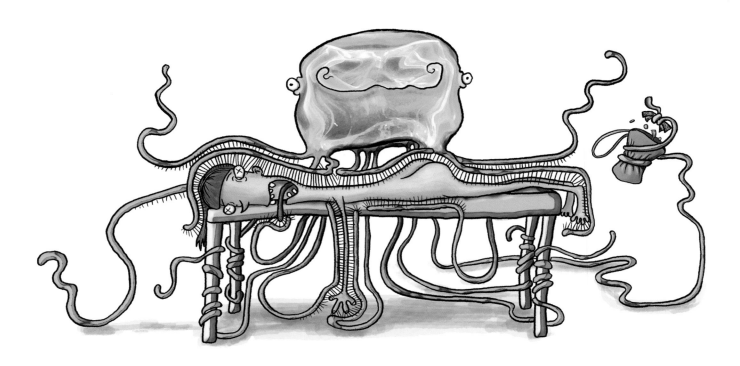

Box jellyfish kill around 100 people worldwide every year. Their tentacles inject their victims with thousands of poisonous darts, which inflict agonizing pain. Thankfully, the pain subsides in a couple of minutes when the victim dies.

K is for Komodo Dragon

PET SCHMO

SALE — Price Reduced!

OPEN

Tiny Dinosaur!

Komodo Dragons will kill you.

Komodo dragons have mauled two people to death since 2007. At 10 feet long and 200 pounds, they are the largest lizards on earth. If you ever find yourself on the receiving end of a tiny dinosaur hug, it is probably because you go out of your way to make bad life choices.

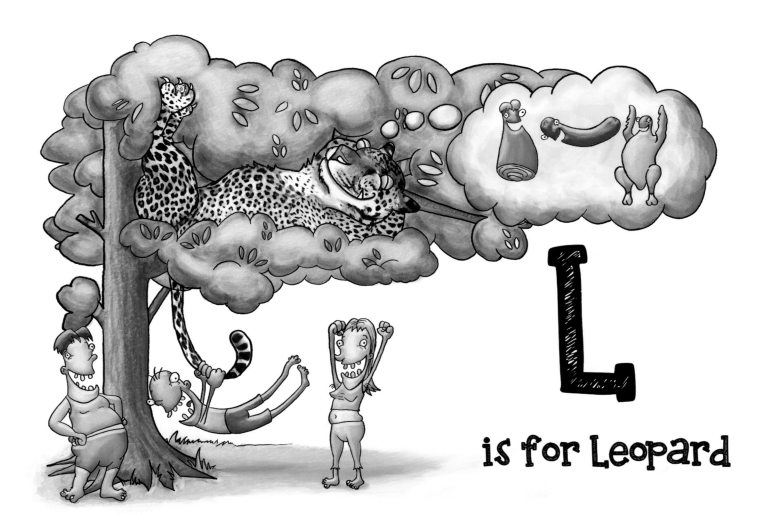

L

is for Leopard

Leopards will kill you.

On the Indian subcontinent from 1875 to 1912, leopards killed almost 12,000 people. Leopards are angry killing machines that spend all daydreaming about what people taste like and all night eating them in trees.

M

is for Mosquito

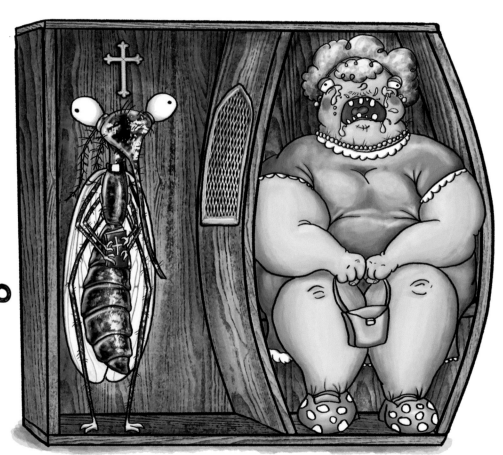

Mosquitoes will kill you.

Mosquitoes are responsible for 600,000 to 1,000,000 deaths every year through the transmission of malaria. Mosquitoes are a reminder that no matter how far society advances, you're never truly safe anywhere.

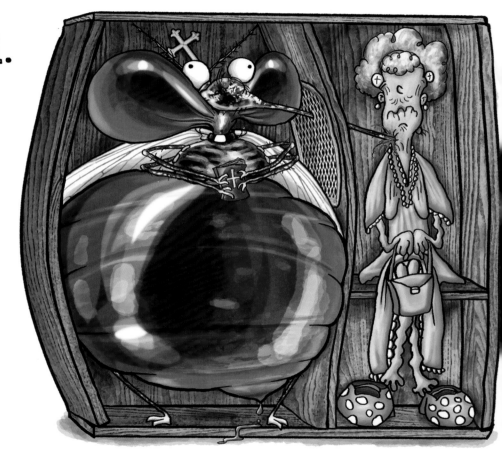

Newts will kill you.

Rough-skinned newts produce a neurotoxin called tetrodotoxin, which induces paralysis and utlimately death upon ingestion. In 1979, a man in Oregon swallowed a rough-skinned newt on a dare and died a few hours later because boys are very stupid.

O is for Octopus

Octopuses will kill you.

About five people suffocate every year in an attempt to eat live baby octopus. Sometimes the grossest thing you do is also the dumbest thing you do, and then the last thing you do.

P

is for
Pufferfish

Pufferfish will kill you.

Fugu, a famous Japanese dish made from the extremely toxic puffer fish, kills a handful of people every year, way down from its peak of 176 deaths in 1958. If you intentionally eat the most poisonous fish on earth and die, people are allowed to laugh at your funeral.

Is for Quail

Quails will kill you.

Coturnism is an illness contracted by migratory quails that have eaten poisonous seeds and can cause death from heart or kidney failure. Humans have known about coturnism since the 4th century BCE, but continue to eat quail because we are hungrier than we are smart.

is for Rattlesnake

Rattlesnakes will kill you.

Rattlesnakes are responsible for the majority of venomous snakebites in the US, resulting in five to six deaths each year. Rattlesnakes also have a big loud rattle that they shake to warn you that you're too close, so if you get bitten, it's kind of your own fault.

S is for Scorpion

Scorpions will kill you.

Scorpions kill more than 3,000 people every year, dwarfing the number of deaths by spider bites. They prefer to hide in dark warm places, like your shoes. There are probably scorpions in all of your shoes right now.

T

is for Tiger

Tigers will kill you.

The Champawat Tiger was a Bengal tiger responsible for killing 436 people in the late nineteenth and early twentieth centuries. You probably don't have 436 friends, but if you did, one tiger could eat all of them if given enough time.

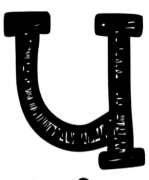

U

is for

Urchin

Urchins will kill you.

The flower urchin is covered in circular flower-like pedicellariae that clamp shut when disturbed and administer toxic venom. Flower urchins are beautiful and will poison you, just like all the pretty people in your life.

V is for Vampire Bat

Vampire Bats will kill you.

In 2010, a 19-year-old man was the first ever recorded death in the US from a vampire bat bite. This number is projected to grow as global warming makes the southern US states more hospitable for the little flying rabies sacks.

W is for Wild Boar

Wild Boars will Kill you.

Wild Boars kill an average of four people worldwide each year. On occasion, they partially eat their human victims in what is widely considered vengeance for bacon.

is for *Xiphias Gladius*

Swordfish will kill you.

In 2015, a swordfish killed a fisherman who had speared it and jumped into the water to retrieve it. In a battle of sharp pointy objects, you're at a distinct advantage if you stay out of the water where the giant fish with a sword on its face can stab you.

Yaks will kill you.

In Tibet, yak dung is used as fuel for indoor cooking stoves. Indoor pollution from cooking and heating stoves kills millions of people every year. Turns out it's dangerous to breathe in burning poop smoke — surprise!

Z is for Zebra

Zebras will kill you.

Zebra attacks in Zoos are surprisingly vicious, resulting in severe injuries and occasional deaths, presumably out of anger that they are always placed last in alphabet books.

Bibliography

"Blowfish Poison Is Toxic." Tokyo Metropolitan Welfare and Health Bureau. Accessed November 15, 2016. http://www.fukushihoken.metro.tokyo.jp/shokuhin/hugu/. This is why you should not eat one.

Bradley, Susan G. and Larry J. Klika. "A Fatal Poisoning from the Oregon Rough-Skinned Newt (Taricha granulosa)." *The Journal of the American Medical Association* 246, no. 3 (1981): 247. doi:10.1001/jama.1981.03320030039026. Ditto on newt eating.

"British Pensioner, 77, Died After Collision with Zebra in African Safari Horror." *The Daily Mail.* Last modified June 17, 2009. http://www.dailymail.co.uk/news/article-1193673/Charging-zebra-killed-British-pensioner-77--African-safari-horror.html. Zebras will murder you, no matter how you pronounce their names.

Brown, Larisa and Michelle Nichols. "Home Fires: The World's Most Lethal Pollution." *The Independent.* Last modified January 23, 2011. https://www.independent.co.uk/life-style/health-and-families/health-news/home-fires-the-worlds-most-lethal-pollution-2192000.html. Read this if you are not currently depressed about the state of the world but would like to be.

Cheng, David. "Scorpion Envenomation." Medscape. Last modified November 28, 2017. https://emedicine.medscape.com/article/168230-overview. If you don't know that scorpions are dangerous, they're living under a rock.

"CJD Surveillance Data 1993-2013." *Creutzfeldt–Jakob Disease International Surveillance Network*, University of Edinburgh. Accessed November 2, 2016. http://www.eurocjd.ed.ac.uk/surveillance%20data%201.html. Hooray numbers!

"First Vampire Bat-Related Death Reported In The U.S." *The Huffington Post.* Last modified December 6, 2017. https://www.huffingtonpost.com/2011/08/11/first-vampire-bat-death-us_n_924996.html. There are worse bloodsucking monsters in the government.

Fox, Stuart. "How Deadly Is the Box Jellyfish?" LiveScience. Last modified April 27, 2010. https://www.livescience.com/6353-deadly-box-jellyfish.html. Spoiler alert: very deadly.

Gruber, Karl. "Poison Dart Frogs Are the Most Poisonous Animals Alive." *BBC.* Last modified April 22, 2015. http://www.bbc.com/earth/story/20150422-the-worlds-most-poisonous-animal. With the exception of your ex.

Hatfield, Amy. "Just How Deadly Is a Wild Boar?" *Grand View Outdoors.* Last modified June 11, 2018. https://www.grandviewoutdoors.com/predator-hunting/hogs/just-deadly-wild-boar/. Wild boars ain't nothing to funk with.

"List of fatal alligator attacks in the United States." *Wikipedia.* Accessed September 20, 2018. https://en.wikipedia.org/wiki/List_of_fatal_alligator_attacks_in_the_United_States. Florida man arrested for throwing an alligator through a drive-thru window."

"Human Elephant Conflict." EleAid. Accessed November 13, 2016. http://www.eleaid.com/elephant-conservation/elephant-death-humans/. They seem nicer in the movies.

Kissel, Joe. "Poison Dart Frogs: Pretty to Look At, but Don't Put Them in Your Mouth." *Interesting Thing of the Day* (blog). Last modified May 13, 2018. http://itotd.com/articles/445/poison-dart-frogs/. This is pretty good advice.

"Komodo Dragon Attacks Terrorize Indonesia Villages." *ABCNews.* Accessed November 4, 2016. https://abcnews.go.com/Technology/story?id=7681841&page=1. Let's all move to Greenland. There are no dragons in Greenland.

Korkmaz, I., Güven Kukul, S. H. Eren, and Z. Dogan. "Quail Consumption Can Be Harmful." *Journal of Emerging Medicine* 41, no. 5 (2011): 499-502. doi: 10.1016/j.jemermed.2008.03.045. Eat more chicken.

Lewis, David C., Elizabeth Metallinos-Katzaras, and Louis E. Grivetti. "Coturnism: Human Poisoning by European Migratory Quail." *Journal of Cultural Geography* 7, no. 2 (1987): 51-65. doi: https://doi.org/10.1080/08873638709478507. Actually, fried chicken is probably more deadly than quail in the long run. Eat more vegetables.

"Meet the World's Deadliest Snake in Safety." *Taronga Conservation Society.* Last modified September 28, 2012. https://taronga.org.au/news/2014-06-04/meet-worlds-deadliest-snake-safety. Or maybe don't tempt fate.

Montgomery, Garrett. "Zebra Attacks Man in White County, Arkansas, Pet Zebra Owner Hospitalized." *The Spreadit.* Last modified March 16, 2015. http://www.thespreadit.com/zebra-attacks-man-white-county-50717/. They won't stop until we're all dead.

"Number of Persons and Cattle Killed in British India by Wild Beasts and Snakes." *Digital South Asia Library.* University of Chicago. Accessed November 13, 2016. http://www.jstor.org/stable/1761601. Leopards are horrifying.

Nuwer, Rachel. "The Most Infamous Komodo Dragon Attacks of the Last 10 Years." Smithsonian.com. Last modified January 24, 2013. https://www.smithsonianmag.com/science-nature/the-most-infamous-komodo-dragon-attacks-of-the-past-10-years-5831048/?no-ist. Not a list you want to end up on.

Nuwer, Rachel. "Mosquitoes Kill More Humans Than Human Murderers Do." Smithsonian.com. Last modified April 30, 2014. https://www.smithsonianmag.com/smart-news/mosquitoes-kill-more-humans-human-murderers-do-180951272/. Our fear priorities are way out of whack.

Oehme, Frederick W. and Daniel E. Keyler. (2007). "Plant and Animal Toxins." In *Principles and Methods of Toxicology*, 5th edition, edited by A. Wallace Hayes, 1012. New York: CRC Press. Street urchins are less deadly, but dirtier.

Lohr, Steve. "One Man's Fugu Is Another's Poison." *The New York Times*, November 29, 1981. Accessed November 12, 2016. https://www.nytimes.com/1981/11/29/travel/one-man-s-fugu-is-another-s-poison.html. One hundred percent of people who don't eat puffer fish die from alternate causes.

Packham, Chris. "Lone Dolphins – Friend or Foe?" *BBC*, BBC, 9 Sept. 2002, www.bbc.co.uk/insideout/south/series1/lone-dolphins.shtml. This one has a happy ending.

Park, Madison, Dayu Zhang, and Elizabeth Landau. "Deadly Giant Hornets Kill 42 in China." *CNN World.* Last modified October 4, 2013. https://www.cnn.com/2013/10/03/world/asia/hornet-attack-china/. Possibly the scariest creature on earth.

Preuss, Andreas, and Tony Marco. "Swordfish Kills Fisherman Who Was Trying to Catch It in Hawaii." *CNN.* Last modified June 1, 2015. https://www.cnn.com/2015/05/30/us/hawaii-swordfish-kills-fisherman/. Stabbed through the heart, and I'm to blame!

Quammen, David. *Monster of God: The Man-Eating Predator in the Jungles of History and the Mind*. New York: Norton, 2003. Seriously though, leopards are not our friends.

Rhoades, Dusty. "Rattlesnakes and Their Bites." DesertUSA. Accessed October 23, 2016. https://www.desertusa.com/reptiles/rattlesnake-bites-spring.html. Hurt.

Riviera, Gloria. "Tracking Giant Hornets That Have Killed at Least 42 People." *ABCNews*. Last modified October 9, 2013. http://abcnews.go.com/International/tracking-giant-hornets-killed-42-people/story?id=20515232. Why are you tracking them? Run away!

Ruane, Michael E. "Local National Zoo Officials Say Zebra Attack Was the Result of Human Error." *The Washington Post*. Last modified December 13, 2013. https://www.washingtonpost.com/local/national-zoo-officials-say-zebra-attack-was-the-result-of-human-error/2013/12/13/636a879c-6410-11e3-aa81-e1dab1360323_story.html?utm_term=.f2cc40854bc7. That's what the Zebras want you to believe.

"Scorpions and Human Beings." ScorpionWorlds. Accessed November 13, 2016. http://www.scorpionworlds.com/scorpions-and-humans/. Should not get married.

"The Most Dangerous and Lethal Food in the World." *The Chopping Block*. Accessed October 23, 2016. http://www.culinary-training.info/blog/the-most-dangerous-and-lethal-food-in-the-world/. Both puffer fish and octopi make this list, along with a bunch of other stuff you shouldn't eat, dummy.

"Tiger and Leopard Attacks in Nepal." *BBC News*. Last modified April 5, 2012. http://www.bbc.com/news/world-asia-17630703. They tried to fight back, but we still destroyed their habitat.

Watts, Anthony. "Breaking Science News: Yak Dung Burning Pollutes Indoor Air of Tibetan Households." *WUWT* (blog). Last modified January 16, 2015. https://wattsupwiththat.com/2015/01/16/breaking-science-news-yak-dung-burning-pollutes-indoor-air-of-tibetan-households/. Still depressing.

"Who, What, Why: How Dangerous Is Bullfighting?" *BBC News*. Last modified May 22, 2014. http://www.bbc.com/news/blogs-magazine-monitor-27520374. Dangerous enough to justify stopping it forever?

"Can Zebras Be Domesticated and Trained to Be Ridden or Draw Carriages Like Horses?" *Quora*. Last modified August 16, 2013. https://www.quora.com/Can-zebras-be-domesticated-and-trained-to-be-ridden-or-draw-carriages-like-horses. No.

Shane Hawley was a writer and performer from Saint Paul, Minnesota. He liked animals a lot more than he liked humans, and he hated animals.

Joel Erkkinen was an artist and film maker from Saint Paul, Minnesota. His true passion was creating a world full of laughter... Looks like it was all just in his head.